# THERE WAS AN OLD LADY WHO SWALLOWED A COW!

by Lucille Colandro
Illustrated by Jared Lee

## Cartwheel Books
an imprint of Scholastic Inc.

In appreciation of the cows and sheep who entertained
David, Dylan, Mia, Michael, Eletta, Lenore, George, and Gene.
— L.C.

In memory of Don Dennis, who many years ago gave this
artist his first job.
— J.L.

Text copyright © 2018 by Lucille Colandro
Illustrations © 2018 by Jared D. Lee Studios

ISBN 978-1-338-27200-0
10 9 8 7 6 5 4 3 2 1          18 19 20 21 22
Printed in U.S.A.     40
First edition, February 2018

There was an old lady who swallowed a cow.
I don't know why she swallowed a cow,
but she did it somehow!

There was an old lady who swallowed some hay.
It made her day to swallow the hay.

She swallowed the hay to feed the cow.
I don't know why she swallowed the cow,
but she did it somehow!

There was an old lady who swallowed a pig.
She danced a jig while she swallowed the pig.

She swallowed the pig to play in the hay.
She swallowed the hay to feed the cow.

I don't know why she swallowed the cow,
but she did it somehow!

There was an old lady who swallowed a duck.
It took some luck to swallow that duck.

She swallowed the duck to chase the pig.
She swallowed the pig to play in the hay.
She swallowed the hay to feed the cow.

I don't know why she swallowed the cow,
but she did it somehow!

There was an old lady who swallowed a horse.
It took some force to swallow that horse.

She swallowed the horse to cheer on the duck.
She swallowed the duck to chase the pig.
She swallowed the pig to play in the hay.

She swallowed the hay to feed the cow.
I don't know why she swallowed the cow,
but she did it somehow!

There was an old lady who swallowed a sheep.
She collapsed in a heap
when she swallowed the sheep.

She swallowed the sheep to sing with the horse.

She swallowed the horse to cheer on the duck.

She swallowed the duck to chase the pig.

She swallowed the pig to play in the hay.

She swallowed the hay to feed the cow.

I don't know why she swallowed the cow,
but she did it somehow!

There was an old lady who swallowed a fiddle.
It was quite the riddle, her swallowing a fiddle.

Just then, a rooster crowed, "Cock-a-doodle-doo!"

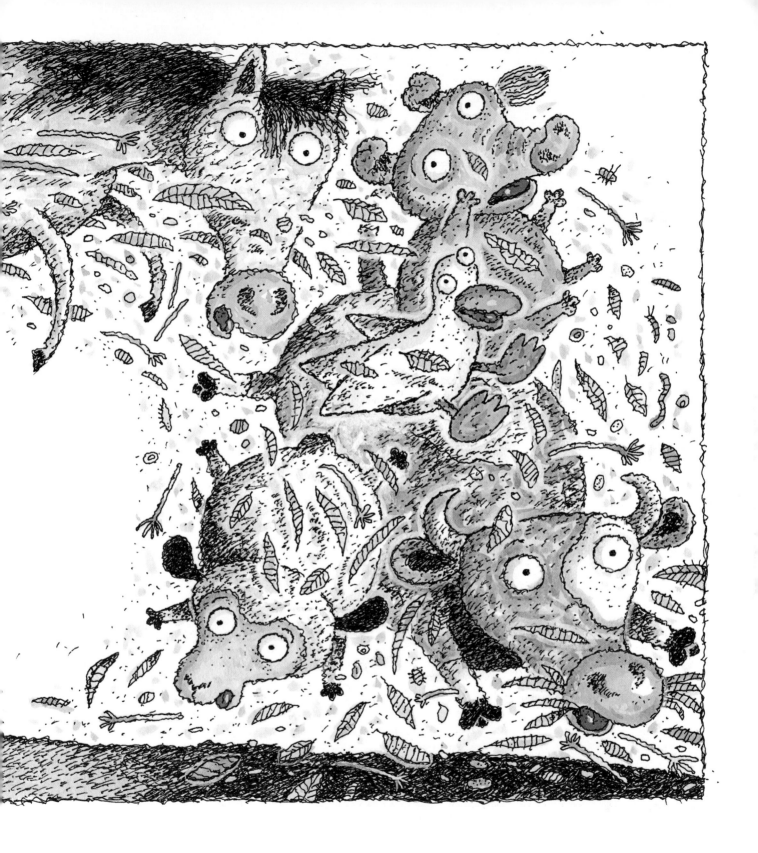

And out flew the animals two by two.

Around the farm, they began to prance . . .

and do-si-do at the Barnyard Square Dance!